FROM JOET
RODGER,
CHRISTMAS '18

D1505625

The Osage Orange Tree

A STORY BY
WILLIAM STAFFORD

Linocut Illustrations by Dennis Cunningham

Afterword by Naomi Shihab Nye

TRINITY UNIVERSITY PRESS
SAN ANTONIO, TEXAS

Published by Trinity University Press
San Antonio, Texas 78212

Text copyright © 1959 by William Stafford, 2014 by the Estate of William
Stafford. Illustrations copyright © 2014 by Dennis Cunningham. Afterword copyright © 2014 by Naomi Shihab Nye.

The publisher gratefully acknowledges the generous support of Scot Sie-
gel and Leah Stenson. Special thanks to William Howe and Joy Bottinelli,
whose gift supported the artwork by Dennis Cunningham.

All rights reserved. No part of this book may be reproduced in any form
or by any electronic or mechanical means, including information storage
and retrieval systems, without permission in writing from the publisher.

Trinity University Press strives to produce its books using methods and
materials in an environmentally sensitive manner. We favor working
with manufacturers that practice sustainable management of all natural
resources, produce paper using recycled stock, and manage forests with
the best possible practices for people, biodiversity, and sustainability. The
press is a member of the Green Press Initiative, a nonprofit program dedi-
cated to supporting publishers in their efforts to reduce their impacts on
endangered forests, climate change, and forest-dependent communities.

The paper used in this publication meets the minimum requirements of
the American National Standard for Information Sciences—Permanence
of Paper for Printed Library Materials, ansi 39.48-1992.

ISBN 978-1-59534-184-6 hardcover
ISBN 978-1-59534-102-0 ebook

CIP data on file at the Library of Congress

18 17 16 15 14   5 4 3 2 1

For Dorothy

CONTENTS

The Osage Orange Tree

Afterword

Naomi Shihab Nye

Biographical Notes

The Osage Orange Tree

On that first day of high school in the prairie town where the tree was, I stood in the sun by the flagpole and watched, but pretended not to watch, the others. They stood in groups and talked and knew each other, all except one—a girl though—in a faded blue dress, carrying a sack lunch and standing near the corner looking everywhere but at the crowd.

I might talk to her, I thought. But of course it was out of the question. That first day was easier when the classes started. Some of the teachers were kind; some were frightening. Some of the students didn't care, but I listened and waited; and at the end of the day I was relieved, less conspicuous from then on.

But that day was not really over. As I hurried to carry my new paper route, I was thinking about how in a strange town, if you are quiet, no one notices, and some may like you, later. I was thinking about this when I reached the north edge of town where the scattering houses dwindle. Beyond them to the north lay just openness, the plains, a big swoop of nothing.

There, at the last house, just as I cut across a lot and threw to the last customer, I saw the girl in the blue dress coming along the street, heading on out of town, carrying books. And she saw me.

"Hello."

"Hello."

And because we stopped we were friends. I didn't know how I could stop, but I didn't hurry on. I stood. There was nothing to do but to act as if I were walking on out too. I had three papers left in the bag, and I frantically began to fold them—box them, was what we called it—for throwing. We had begun to walk and talk. The girl was timid; I became more bold. Not much, but a little.

"Have you gone to school here before?" I asked.

"Yes, I went here last year."

A long pause. A meadowlark sitting on a fencepost hunched his wings and flew. I kicked through the dust of the road. I began to look ahead. Where could we be walking to? I couldn't be walking just because I wanted to be with her. Fortunately, there was one more house, a gray house by a sagging barn, set two hundred yards from the road. "I thought I'd see if I could get a customer here," I said, waving toward the house.

"That's where I live."

"Oh."

We were at the dusty car tracks that turned off the road to the house. The girl stopped. There was a tree at that corner, a straight but little tree with slim branches and shiny dark leaves.

"I could take a paper tonight to see if my father wants to buy it."

A great relief, this. What could I have said to her parents? I held out a paper, dropped it, picked it up, brushing off the dust. "No, here's a new one"—a great action, putting the dusty paper in the bag over my shoulder and pulling out a fresh one. When she took the paper we stood there for a minute. The wind was coming in over the grass. She looked out with a tranquil expression.

She walked away past the tree, and I went quickly back toward town. Could anyone in the houses have been watching us? I looked back once. The girl was standing on the small bridge halfway to her house. I hurried on.

The next day at school I didn't ask her whether her father wanted to take the paper. When the others were there I wouldn't say anything. I stood with the boys. In American history the students could choose their seats, and I saw that she was too quiet and plainly dressed for many to notice her. But I crowded in with the boys, pushing one aside, scrambling for a seat by the window.

That night I came to the edge of town. Two papers were left, and I walked on out. The meadowlark was there. By some reeds in a ditch by the road a dragonfly—snake feeders, we called them—glinted. The sun was going down, and the plains were stretched out and lifted, some way, to the horizon. Could I go on up to the house? I didn't think so, but I walked on. Then, by the tree where her road turned off, she was standing. She was holding her books. More confused than ever, I stopped.

"My father will take the paper," she said.

She told me always to leave the paper at the foot of the tree. She insisted on that, saying their house was too far; and it is true that I was far off my route, a long way, half a mile out of my territory. But I didn't think of that.

And so we were acquainted. What I remember best in that town is those evening walks to the tree. Every night—or almost every night—the girl was there.

Evangeline was her name. We didn't say much. On Friday night of the first week she gave me a dime, the cost of the paper. It was a poor newspaper, by the way, cheap, sensational, unreliable.

I never went up to her house. She and I never talked together at school. But all the time we knew each other; we just happened to meet. Every evening.

There was a low place in the meadow by that corner. The fall rains made a pond there, and in the evenings sometimes ducks would be coming in—a long line with set wings down the wind, and then a turn, and a skimming glide to the water. The wind would be blowing and the grass bent down. The evenings got colder and colder. The wind was cold.

As winter came on the time at the tree was dimmer, but not dark. In the winter there was snow. The pond was frozen over; all the plains were white. I had to walk down the ruts of the road and leave the paper in the crotch of the tree, sometimes, when it was cold. The wind made a sound through the black branches. But usually, even on cold evenings, Evangeline was there.

At school we played ball at noon—the boys did. And I got acquainted. I learned that Evangeline's brother was janitor at the school. A big dark boy he was—a man, middle-aged I thought at the time. He didn't ever let on that he knew me. I would see him sweeping the halls, bent down, slow. I would see him and Evangeline take their sack lunches over to the south side of the building.

Once I slipped away from the ball game and went over there, but he looked at me so steadily, without moving, that I pretended to be looking for a book, and quickly went back, and got in the game and struck out.

You don't know about those winters, and especially that winter. Those were the dust years. Wheat was away down in price. Everyone was poor—poor in a way that you can't understand. I made two dollars a week, or something like that, on my paper route. I could tell about working for ten cents an hour—and then not getting paid; about families that ate wheat, boiled, for their main food, and burned wheat for fuel. You don't know how it would be. All through that hard winter I carried a paper to the tree by the pond, in the evening, and gave it to Evangeline.

In the cold weather Evangeline wore a heavier dress, a dark, straight, heavy dress, under a thick black coat. Outdoors she wore a knitted cap that fastened under her chin. She was dressed this way when we met and she took the paper. The reeds were broken now. The meadowlark was gone.

And then came the spring. I have forgotten to tell just how Evangeline looked. She was of medium height, and slim. Her face was pale, her forehead high, her eyes blue. Her tranquil face I remember well. I remember her watching the wind come in over the grass. Her dress was long, her feet small.

I can remember her by the tree, with her books, or walking on up the road toward her house and stopping on the bridge halfway up there, but she didn't wave, and I couldn't tell whether she was watching me or not. I always looked back as I went over the rise toward town.

And I can remember her in the room at school. She came into American history one spring day, the first really warm day. She had changed from the dark heavy dress to the dull blue one of the last fall; and she had on a new belt, a gray belt, with blue stitching along the edges. As she passed in front of Jane Wright, a girl who sat on the front row, I heard Jane say to the girl beside her, "Why look at Evangeline. . . . That old dress of hers has a new belt!"

"Stop a minute, Evangeline," Jane said, "let me see your new dress."

Evangeline stopped and looked uncertainly at Jane and blushed.

"It's just made over," she said, "It's just. . . ."

"It's cute, Dear," Jane said; and as Evangeline went on Jane nudged her friend in the ribs and the friend smothered a giggle.

Well, that was a good year. Commencement time came, and—along with the newspaper job—I had the task of preparing for finals and all. One thing, I wasn't a student who took part in the class play or anything like that. I was just one of the boys—twenty-fourth in line to get my diploma.

And graduation was bringing an end to my paper carrying. My father covered a big territory in our part of the state, selling farm equipment; and we were going to move at once to a town seventy miles south. Only because of my finishing the school year had we stayed till graduation.

I had taught another boy my route, always leaving him at the end and walking on out, by myself, to the tree. I didn't really have to go around with him that last day, the day of graduation, but I was going anyway.

At the graduation exercises that May afternoon, I wore my brown Sunday suit. My mother was in the audience. It was a heavy day. The girls had on new dresses. But I didn't see *her*.

I suppose that I did deserve old man Sutton's "Shhh!" as we lined up to march across the stage, but I for the first time in the year forgot my caution, and asked Jane where Evangeline was. She shrugged, and I could see for myself that she was not there.

We marched across the stage; our diplomas were ours; our parents filed out; to the strains of a march on the school organ we trailed to the hall. I unbuttoned my brown suit coat, stuffed the diploma in my pocket, and sidled out of the group and upstairs.

Evangeline's brother was emptying wastebaskets at the far end of the hall. I sauntered toward him and stopped. I didn't know what I wanted to say. Unexpectedly, he solved my problem. Stopping in his work, holding a partly empty wastebasket over the canvas sack he wore over his shoulder, he stared at me, as if almost to say something.

"I noticed that . . . your sister wasn't here," I said. The noise below was dwindling. The hall was quiet, an echoey place; my voice sounded terribly loud. He emptied the rest of the wastebasket and shifted easily. He was a man, in big overalls. He stared at me.

"Evangeline couldn't come," he said. He stopped, looked at me again, and said, "She stole."

"Stole?" I said. "Stole what?" He shrugged and went toward the next wastebasket, but I followed him.

"She stole the money from her bank . . . the money she was to use for her graduation dress," he said. He walked stolidly on, and I stopped.

He deliberately turned away as he picked up the next wastebasket. But he said something else, half to himself. "You knew her. You talked to her . . . I know." He walked away.

I hurried downstairs and outside. The new carrier would have the papers almost delivered by now; so I ran up the street toward the north. I took a paper from him at the end of the street and told him to go back. I didn't pay any more attention to him.

No one was at the tree, and I turned, for the first time, up the road to the house. I walked over the bridge and on up the narrow, rutty tracks. The house was gray and lopsided. The ground of the yard was packed; nothing grew there. By the back door, the door to which the road led, there was a grayish-white place on the ground where the dishwater had been thrown. A gaunt shepherd dog trotted out growling.

And the door opened suddenly, as if someone had been watching me come up the track. A woman came out—a woman stern-faced, with a shawl over her head and a dark lumpy dress on—came out on the back porch and shouted, "Go 'way, go 'way! We don't want no papers!"

She waved violently with one hand, holding the other on her shawl, at her throat. She coughed so hard that she leaned over and put her hand against one of the uprights of the porch. Her face was red. She glanced toward the barn and leaned toward me. "Go 'way!"

Behind me a meadowlark sang. Over all the plains swooped the sky. The land was drawn up somehow toward the horizon.

I stood there, half-defiant, half-ashamed. The dog continued to growl and to pace around me, stiff-legged, his tail down. The windows of the house were all blank, with blinds drawn. I couldn't say anything.

I stood a long time and then, lowering the newspaper I had held out, I stood longer, waiting, without thinking of what to do. The meadowlark bubbled over again, but I turned and walked away, looking back once or twice. The old woman continued to stand, leaning forward, her head out. She glanced at the barn, but didn't call out any more.

My heels dug into the grayish place where the dishwater had been thrown; the dog skulked along behind.

At the bridge, halfway to the road, I stopped and looked back. The dog was lying down again; the porch was empty; and the door was closed. Turning the other way, I looked toward town. Near me stood our ragged little tree—an Osage orange tree it was. It was feebly coming into leaf, green all over the branches, among the sharp thorns. I hadn't wondered before how it grew there, all alone, in the plains country, neglected. Over our pond some ducks came slicing in.

Standing there on the bridge, still holding the folded—boxed—newspaper, that worthless paper, I could see everything. I looked out along the road to town. From the bridge you would see the road going away, to where it went over the rise.

Glancing around, I flipped that last newspaper under the bridge and then bent far over and looked where it had gone.

There they were—a pile of boxed newspapers, all of them thrown in a heap, some new, some worn and weathered, by rain, by snow.

AFTERWORD

William Stafford may not have written many stories in his life, favoring poems and essays, but "The Osage Orange Tree," this rare example, rings with the stark perfection of a master's love and care.

Stafford wrote about common people in a humble place, doing unspectacular, daily things. A teenage boy goes to high school and delivers newspapers. He notices others. In Stafford's own youth he had lived these streets, through spartan times, in small-town middle America, where a boy's after-school job might be integral to his family's livelihood.

As ever, with characteristic graciousness and ease, he transports us to that grounded landscape. No flash, no drama. He invites us into a tough but enticing world, giving us a cadence and atmosphere to bask in—and then we may entertain the questions that bubble up around the margins of his seemingly simple story: Why these particular details? Did he really know that girl? Is she one of those people we all imagine we see, off to the edge of the picture? Did he really wonder about her then, when young, or only when looking back on that precious, difficult, finite time?

Stafford writes the story in compact unembellished increments. Its sections feel like days passing. The boy in the story keeps showing up for work. Always, he shows up.

This could remind us of Stafford's devotion to writing, his lifelong daily allegiance to early morning margins, the horizontal sacred scrawling time on the couch, before he went to work. He knew that showing up for writing would help thoughts and words continue to flow onto pages, rolling forward with mystery and possibility, but always rolling.

In fact, that whole metaphor of rolling text might parallel the rolled newspapers the boy in "The Osage Orange Tree" finds under the bridge, after he has been sent away from Evangeline's house, words tossed aside while still rolled up, unread, under the path they have been walking. Such a stunning, lonesome ending this is—it jolts the reader's breath.

What happens to us? We come so close to connecting. Sometimes, for a short time, when we're lucky, things work out. All of William Stafford's life, he believed there were ways human beings find a hinge among themselves that swings a door wide open. We find a hinge in language and it helps us. Something small but shining—a gaze that joins us for a moment—

words that touch in a new way—a pause in the stream of things—the tiniest unnoticed scrap of presence or beauty waiting almost unwitnessed by the side of any road. Waiting under the bridge, the stories we didn't bother to write. The friends we will never have another chance to make.

Stafford believed in so many potent, magnificent things in his poems, but he never gave false assurance that days or tales would work out perfectly. Rather, he offered the widest, closest, most balanced gaze of any twentieth-century poet. He scanned the horizon and told us the truth.

Characteristically and magically, the Osage orange tree is a silent witness in this story. It stands at the spot where lives do and do not connect: "a straight but little tree with slim branches and shiny dark leaves." Around it, everything does and does not happen. William Stafford, with his fine instinctive touch, knew just how much to tell.

Now we see that he might easily have been a writer of stories all his life instead of a poet. Maybe his poems were the unrolling of those pages under the bridge.

—*Naomi Shihab Nye*

William Stafford, one of America's most widely read poets, graduated from Liberal High School in southwestern Kansas at the depth of the Great Depression, in the era in which this story is set. For a time in those days, his father was out of work, and young William's paper route was the only source of family income.

He attended the University of Kansas, receiving a B.A. in English. His career as a poet and educator was shaped by his experience of hard physical labor and by the discipline and cooperative ethos of Civilian Public Service camp life as a conscientious objector during World War II, where he began his lifelong habit of writing in the early hours each day, before first light.

William Stafford published some fifty volumes of poetry, including *Traveling Through the Dark*, which won the National Book Award. In 1970 he was named Consultant in Poetry to the Library of Congress. He taught for thirty years at Lewis & Clark College in Oregon, and traveled the world to share his poetry.

Dennis Cunningham is a highly regarded printmaker with a long history of exhibitions, awards, public art works, and publications, and has taught at Marylhurst University since 1986. According to Cunningham, his work is grounded in "my awareness as a child that I wanted to be an artist. Everything I have done in the past forty years stems from that optimistic vision of my place in the world. I continue to hold that childhood desire: it nourishes me every day I work."

Naomi Shihab Nye, a close friend of William Stafford, describes herself as a "wandering poet" and has spent four decades leading writing workshops and inspiring students of all ages across the United States and beyond. Nye was born to a Palestinian father and an American mother, and grew up in St. Louis, Jerusalem, and San Antonio. Author or editor of thirty-three books, she is currently a chancellor of the Academy of American Poets and lives near San Antonio's beloved little river.

As part of its hundredth anniversary celebration in 1959, the State of Oregon held four statewide literary contests—one each for the general public and for college and university students, in the categories of poetry and short fiction—and published the winning entries in *The Oregon Centennial Anthology, 1859–1959*. William Stafford won first prize in both of the competitions for the public, for his poem "Memorials of a Tour Around Mt. Hood" and for his story "The Osage Orange Tree."

This first edition of "The Osage Orange Tree" as a stand-alone volume is published on the occasion of William Stafford's own centennial year, 2014. It has been produced as a collaboration between editor Kim Stafford, artist Dennis Cunningham, and book designer John Laursen, working in concert with Barbara Ras, director of Trinity University Press, and Sarah Nawrocki, managing editor. Torey Browne assisted Mr. Cunningham with the editioning of the original linocut prints. The typeface is Stone Serif, and the paper is Finch Vanilla Smooth. The books have been printed and bound by RR Donnelley.